TIDY
TITCH

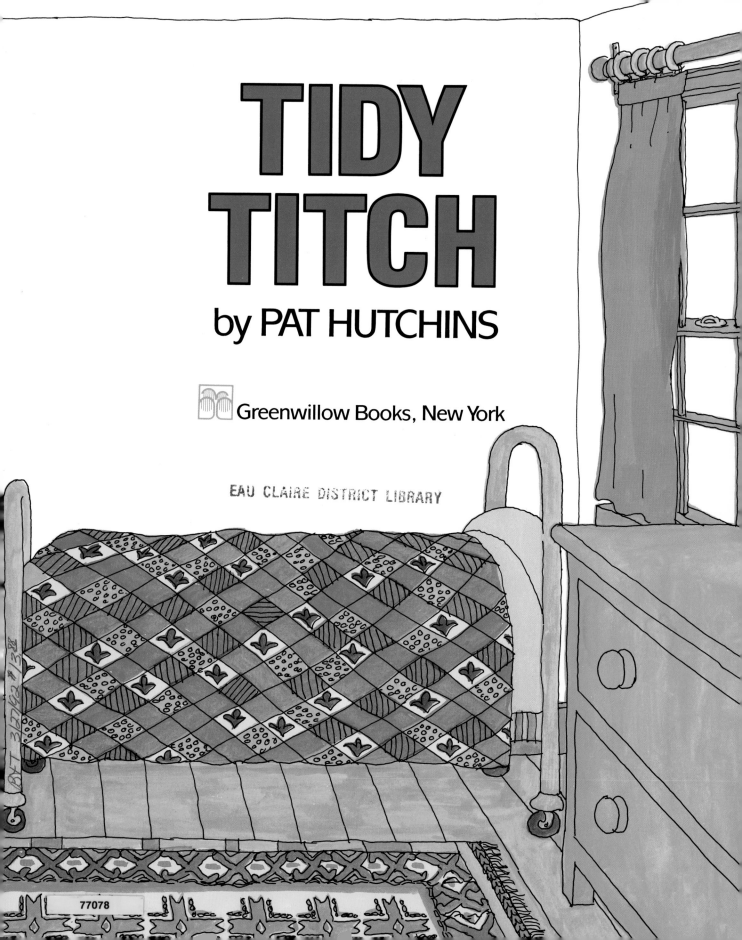

TIDY
TITCH

by PAT HUTCHINS

Greenwillow Books, New York

Watercolor paints and pen-and-ink
were used for the full-color art.
The text type is Mixage Medium.

Printed in Singapore by Tien Wah Press
First Edition   10 9 8 7 6 5 4 3 2 1

Library of Congress Cataloging-in-Publication Data
Hutchins, Pat (date)
Tidy Titch / by Pat Hutchins.
p.   cm.
Summary: Titch helps his older brother and
sister clean their rooms.
ISBN 0-688-09963-7. ISBN 0-688-09964-5 (lib. bdg.)
[1. Cleanliness—Fiction. 2. Orderliness—Fiction.
3. Brothers and sisters—Fiction.]   I. Title.
PZ7.H96165Th   1991
[E]—dc20   90-38483   CIP   AC

FOR DAISY GOUNDRY

TIDY
TITCH

"How tidy Titch's room is,"
said Mother to Peter and Mary.
"And how messy your rooms are.
I think you should tidy them up."

"I'll help," said Titch
as Mother went downstairs.

"I think I'll throw this
 dollhouse out," said Mary,
"and these toys.
 I'm too old for them!"
"I'm not," said Titch.
"I'll have them!"

And Titch carried the dollhouse
and the toys to his room.

"I think I'll throw that old
space suit out," said Peter,
"and that cowboy outfit.
They're much too small for me!"
"They're not too small for me!"
said Titch. "I'll have them!"

And Titch carried the space suit
and the cowboy outfit to his room.

"My room is still untidy," said Mary.
"I think I'll get rid of this broken carriage
   and these old games.
   I've played them hundreds of times!"

"I haven't," said Titch.
"I'll have them!"

And Titch took the carriage
and old games to his room.

"My room is still a mess," said Peter.
"I think I'll get rid of
    these old toys. I don't play
    with them any more!"
"I will!" said Titch.
"I'll have them!"

And Titch carried the old toys to his room.

"How neat your rooms are!" said Mother
when she came back upstairs.

"I thought Titch was going to help you."

"He did," said Peter and Mary.

Since the publication of *Rosie's Walk* in 1968, reviewers on both sides of the Atlantic have been loud in their praise of Pat Hutchins's work.

Among her popular picture books are *What Game Shall We Play?; Where's the Baby?* (an *SLJ* Best Book of the Year); *The Doorbell Rang* (an ALA Notable Book); *You'll Soon Grow into Them, Titch*; and *The Wind Blew* (winner of the 1974 Kate Greenaway Medal). For older readers she has written several novels, including *The House That Sailed Away, The Curse of the Egyptian Mummy,* and *Rats!*

Pat Hutchins, her husband, Laurence, and their sons, Morgan and Sam, live in London, England.